# THE SPONGEBOB SQUAREPANTS™ ORACLE

## ·DAVID· LEWMAN

POCKET BOOKS
New York   London   Toronto   Sydney   Singapore   Bikini Bottom

An *Original* Publication of POCKET BOOKS

POCKET BOOKS, a division of Simon & Schuster, Inc.
1230 Avenue of the Americas, New York, NY 10020

ISBN: 0-7434-8316-2

First Pocket Books trade paperback printing November 2003

10 9 8 7 6 5 4 3 2 1

POCKET and colophon are registered trademarks of Simon & Schuster, Inc.

Design by Red Herring Design/NYC
Cover art by Gregg Schigiel

Manufactured in the United States of America

For information regarding special discounts for bulk purchases, please contact Simon & Schuster Special Sales at 1-800-456-6798 or business@simonandschuster.com.

# HOW TO USE THE SPONGEBOB SQUAREPANTS ORACLE

You've got questions. Luckily, SpongeBob and his friends in Bikini Bottom
have answers, all neatly contained in this oracle book.

## HOW TO USE SPONGEBOB'S ORACLE BOOK

1. **Make sure you're on dry land. This book was not designed to be
used underwater. (The pages get all soggy.)**

2. **Think of a yes/no question you need the answer to. If you already
know the answer, there's really no point in asking the book.**

3. **Pick up the book, concentrating on your question. If you're already
holding the book, you can skip this step.**

4. **Resist the urge to go jellyfishing.**

5. **Ask your question out loud, unless it's really embarrassing.**

6. **Rub your fingers along the edges of the book's pages until it feels right to stop.**

7. **STOP!**

8. **Open the book to the page you stopped at. Read what it says.
That's the answer to your question!**

NOTE: **Some pages let you know that the book wasn't quite ready to answer your
question. Simply wait a little while (approximately the amount of time it takes to
eat a Krabby Patty), then ask your question again, following the instructions above.**

ANOTHER NOTE: **Some answers are very clear. Some aren't. You may have to
interpret the answers, just as you interpret a fortune cookie.**

ONE LAST NOTE: **This book tastes nothing like a fortune cookie, so don't eat it,
no matter what Patrick says.**

# Sounds great!

SpongeBob SquarePants

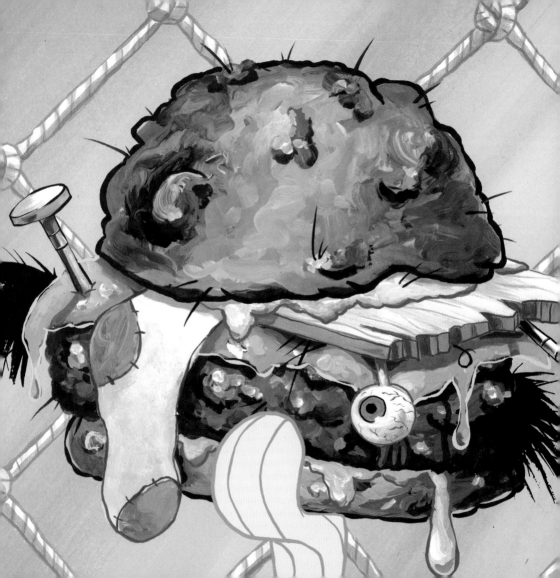

Aargh, that sickens me.

Mr. Krabs

ALL YOU HAVE TO DO IS ANSWER THE PHONE.

SpongeBob SquarePants

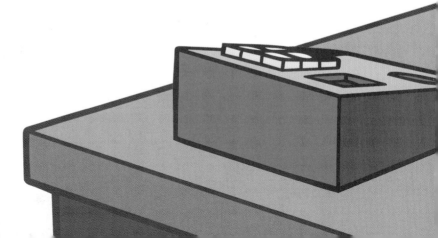

Hey, with those arms, you'll do great!

Sandy Cheeks

RULES of the ROAD

If one wishes to be a good noodle, one must behave like a good noodle.

Mrs. Puff

Oh, i doubt that, my little shrimp boat.

Mr. Krabs

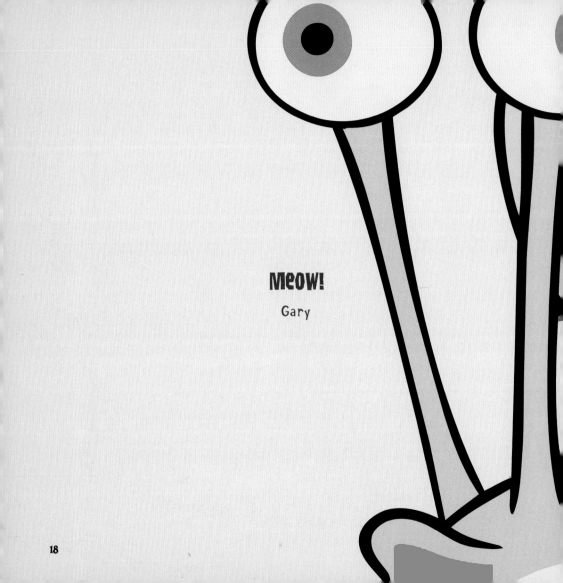

Meow!

Gary

I can't understand anything.

Patrick Star

Get out of my head! Leave my brain alone!

SpongeBob SquarePants

YOU CAN DO ANYTHING YOU WANT.

SpongeBob SquarePants

If you try it, you'll love it.

SpongeBob SquarePants

# Is it time already for you to ruin my day?

Squidward Tentacles

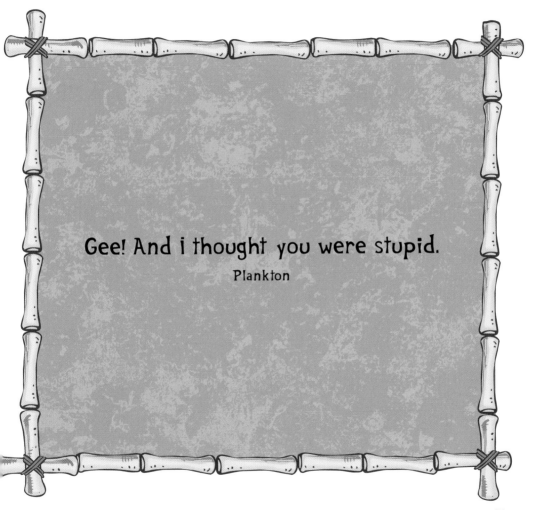

Gee! And i thought you were stupid.

Plankton

Yeah! Ride 'em, cowboy!

Sandy Cheeks

# YOU WON'T BE SORRY.

SpongeBob SquarePants

# I don't think so.

Magic Conch Shell

## Response: Why don't you ask me later?

Robot SpongeBob SquarePants

WHATEVER YOU NORMALLY DO,
TODAY YOU DO THE OPPOSITE!

SpongeBob SquarePants

You must have coral wedged in your frontal lobe.

Squidward Tentacles

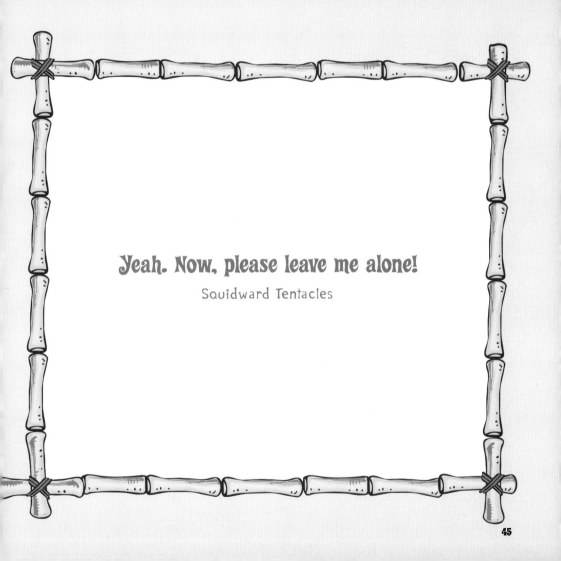

Yeah. Now, please leave me alone!

Squidward Tentacles

We already *played* Babble Like an idiot.

SpongeBob SquarePants

Listen here, you little barnacle. No one, and i mean NO ONE, can ever know about this. it'll be the end of you, it'll be the end of me, and worst of all, it'll be the end of *me!*

Mr. Krabs

**Oh, sure, right. Whatever.
Like that'll ever happen.**

Squidward Tentacles

This is a very delicate situation. It must be handled with great care and sensitivity. RUN!

SpongeBob SquarePants

HA HA HA HA HA! That's a good one!

Patrick Star

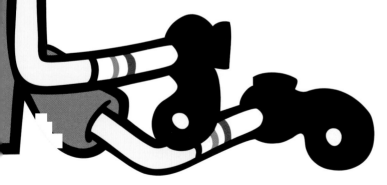

Not even in your dreams.

Mrs. Puff

SOMETIMES WE HAVE TO GO DEEP INSIDE
OURSELVES TO SOLVE OUR PROBLEMS.

Patrick Star

I would love to sit here and play Twenty Questions with you, but I've got only one minute until inspection.

SpongeBob SquarePants

# Wow! Now THAT'S a good idea!

SpongeBob SquarePants

**Never ever never never ever ever never.**

SpongeBob SquarePants

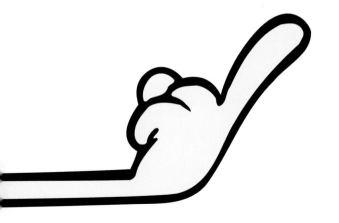

Why don't you ask my behind? That is,
if you can catch it!

Sandy Cheeks

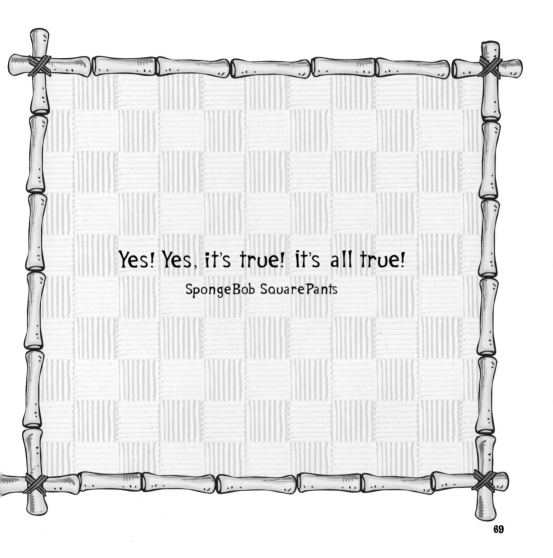

Yes! Yes, it's true! it's all true!

SpongeBob SquarePants

Nothing's too good for you, my prickly peach.

Mr. Krabs

**You're gonna hafta not do that. And stop starin' at me with them big ol' eyes.**

The Flying Dutchman

**I guess all dreams aren't meant to come true. Back to reality.**

SpongeBob SquarePants

**It feels nice to do good.**

SpongeBob SquarePants

Always thinking about yourself.
Get out there and stall!

Mr. Krabs

**Wrong! Wrong! Wrong! Nope! Naw! Negatory! Nyet!**

SpongeBob SquarePants

**Okay, but this is your last chance!**

Plankton

# you poor ugly thing, you.

Patrick Star

Not on your life, sport.

Squidward Tentacles

What you need to do is surround yourself with muscular tough guys who will do whatever you say.

Plankton's Computer Wife, Karen

**That would be so cool!**

SpongeBob SquarePants

The inner machinations of my mind are an enigma.

Patrick Star

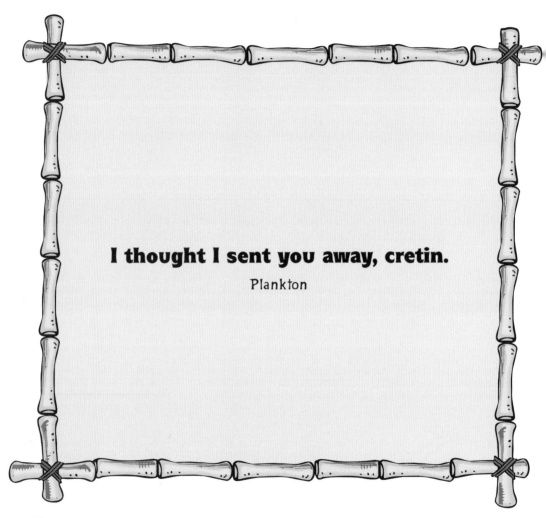

**I thought I sent you away, cretin.**

Plankton

# THIS'LL BE *NO PROBLEMO!*

SpongeBob SquarePants

*I'm running this quiz show! I'll ask the questions!*

SpongeBob SquarePants

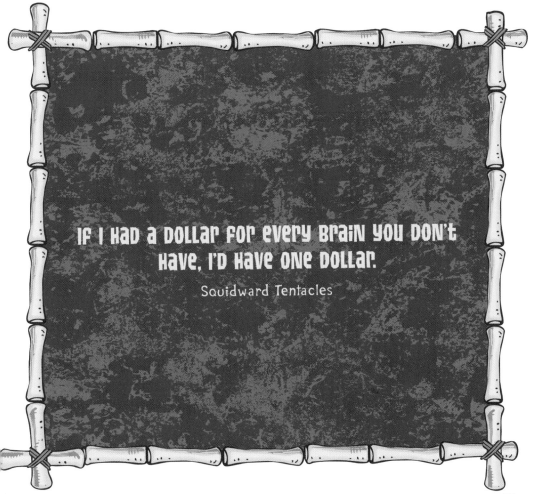

IF I HAD A DOLLAR FOR EVERY BRAIN YOU DON'T HAVE, I'D HAVE ONE DOLLAR.

Squidward Tentacles

**Remember: When in doubt, pinkie out.**

Patrick Star

Have i ever not been right?

Patrick Star

A man's gotta do what a man's gotta do!

SpongeBob SquarePants

You're going to get in trouble.

SpongeBob SquarePants

You had your chance and you Failed.
You have to stop living in the past.

Patrick Star

It's money that makes the world go round, boy!
It's money that keeps your pants square!
It's money that keeps Squidward in frilly soap!
Nothing in all the seven seas could matter more!

Mr. Krabs

How can you be so naive?

SpongeBob SquarePants

Work hard, and no goofing off!
Mrs. Puff

# Never! That's completely idiotic!

Plankton

119

# DON'T WORRY. THERE'S NO DANGER.

SpongeBob SquarePants.

you know what they say—
curiosity salted the snail.

SpongeBob SquarePants

There's something i've been wanting to say
to you since the day we met: Good-bye.

Squidward Tentacles

# Yes! No, wait-uh, no.

Patrick Star

That's creepy.

SpongeBob SquarePants

**Yeah, verily. Now, let's play a nice wholesome game of Eels and Escalators.**

SpongeBob SquarePants

# can we talk about this another time?

Sandy Cheeks

Gotta think! Gotta think! Gotta think!
Gotta run around and think! Gotta run
around and think at the same time!
Gotta think! Gotta have a plan!
Gotta think, think, think!

SpongeBob SquarePants

**Puh-lease tell me this isn't a joke!**

Squidward Tentacles

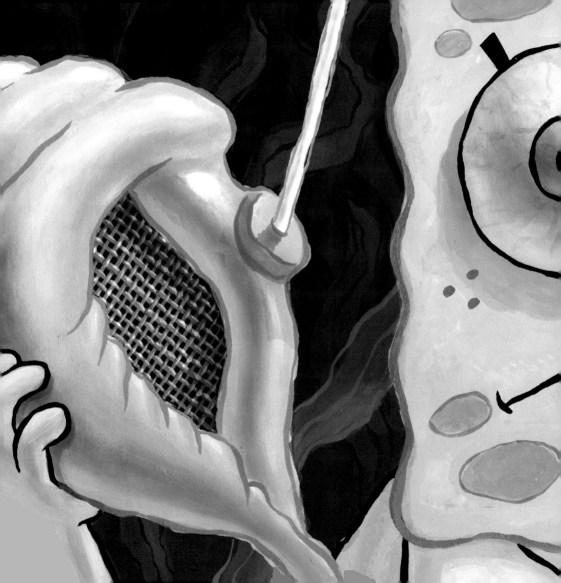

Maybe someday.

Magic Conch Shell

## we'll see about that!

SpongeBob SquarePants

You're nuthin' but pure evil, just like the newspaper comics.

Sandy Cheeks

Don't give up!

SpongeBob SquarePants

**Do exactly as I do.**

SpongeBob SquarePants

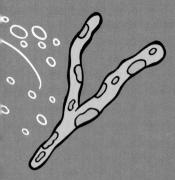

**Tell you what, half-pint,
why don't you ask me later?**

SpongeBob SquarePants

# Life is just two kinds of ice cream.

Mrs. Puff

Just do what i do when i have problems...SCREAM!

Patrick Star

You can do anything you want!

SpongeBob SquarePants

That's it! i QUiT!

Squidward Tentacles

**It's all about finger strength, baby.**

SpongeBob SquarePants

# Keep trying!

SpongeBob SquarePants

**Let's not get carried away.**

Plankton

That's an easy one! You just...
just...let's see. if it's, uh, if it's
January with ...with vanilla
pudding...you...uh...pass?

Mr. Krabs

Never! Ha Ha! Never! Never!

SpongeBob SquarePants

**It's not worth it.**

Plankton

Stupidity isn't a virus, but it sure is spreadin' like one.

Sandy Cheeks

Yes—yes! Whatever!
But you have to promise
not to tell anyone.

Squidward Tentacles

# Heavens to Betsy—No!

Mr. Krabs

**We already talked about that, remember?**

SpongeBob SquarePants

**Do it because I told you to!**

Plankton

Everybody loves pie!

SpongeBob SquarePants

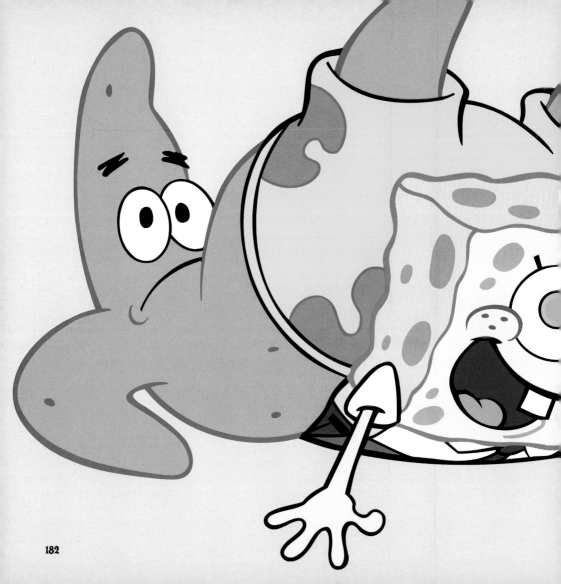

**It would seem we have reached an impasse.**

Patrick Star

184

That makes me feel all wiggly!

SpongeBob SquarePants

185

it's still a mystery!

SpongeBob SquarePants

You missed your chance! You've gotta be aggressive to get the things you want!

Plankton

# OH, YEAH, SURE. NO PROBLEM.

SpongeBob SquarePants

All ye must do is tend to my every whim
and tickle my fancy on demand.

Squidward Tentacles

Life's like a bucket of wood shavings, except for
when the shavings are in a pail–
then it's like a *pail* of wood shavings.

SpongeBob SquarePants

I'm sure that by tomorrow this whole ugly mess will be a funny memory.

SpongeBob SquarePants

**We used to beat people up for saying things like that. Everything's all topsy-turvy now.**

Mr. Krabs

Barnacles, what is this?
Twenty Questions
or something?

SpongeBob SquarePants

I don't know--something still doesn't feel right.

SpongeBob SquarePants

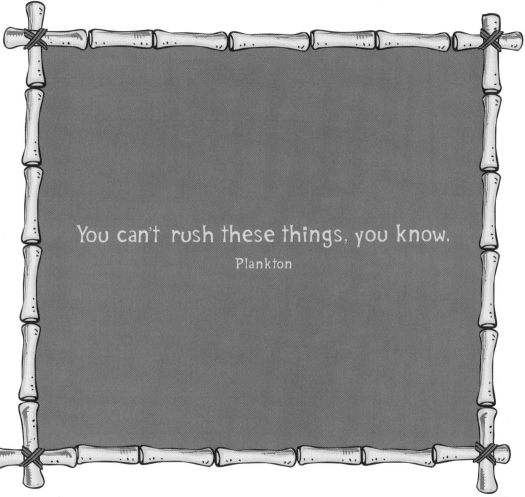

You can't rush these things, you know.

Plankton

208

Wait 'til i finish my ice cream!

SpongeBob SquarePants

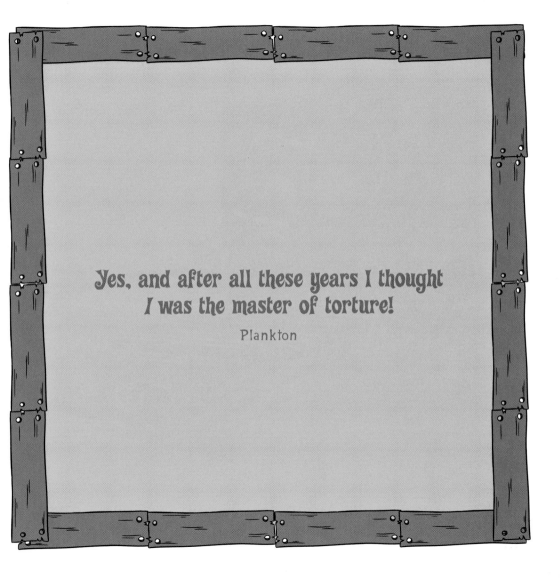

IF EVERYONE COULD JUST TAKE A SEAT ON THE COUCH, PLEASE, WHILE I SORT THIS OUT. THANK YOU.

SpongeBob SquarePants

You are strong! Through your strength
you shall overcome!

SpongeBob SquarePants

Tell you what—you've caught me in a good mood. I'll humor you. Go on! Go out there and act smart For everyone.

Patrick Star

You're too soft!

Plankton

It's only going to take one more year!
One more year! One more super-duper year!
One more super-spectacular, extra-magical,
extra-fantastical year!

SpongeBob SquarePants

Days like today come once, maybe twice, in a lifetime. Savor every moment.

SpongeBob SquarePants

**DO NOT DISTURB! THAT MEANS YOU!**

Sandy Cheeks

225

We all gotta laugh at ourselves once in a while.
i do it all the time!

SpongeBob SquarePants

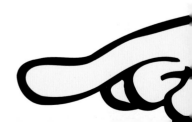

Forget it! I guess you don't have what it takes
to be a stand-up guy.

Plankton

**That's crazy talk!**

Sandy Cheeks

You gotta learn to roll with the punches, go with the Flow. And don't bring anything on a boat that you ain't prepared to lose.

Mr. Krabs

you know, you worry too much.

Patrick Star

Somebody oughta teach you some manners.

SpongeBob SquarePants

You been messing with the bull—
now here come the horns!

Sandy Cheeks

What's that supposed to be?
Some kind of stupid secret code?

Squidward Tentacles

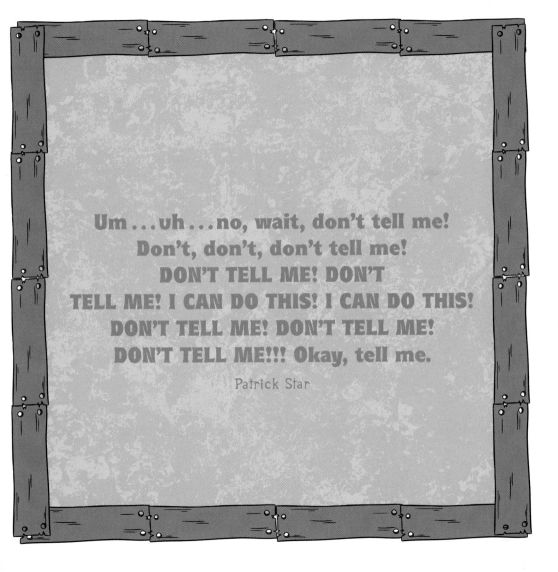

i don't want to talk about it.

Plankton

# Maybe scallops will fly out of my pants!

Mr. Krabs

**Look at yourself. You're losing your bluish glow! Stop worrying so much!**

Squidward Tentacles

**Nice guys finish last! Only aggressive people conquer the world!**

Plankton

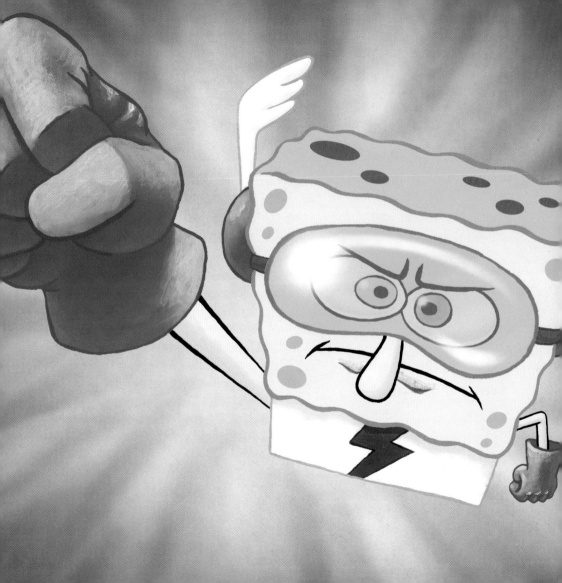

It's a cold, cold world out there. No one's going to serve you happiness on a silver platter.

SpongeBob SquarePants

The shell knows all!

Patrick Star

I DiDN't realize it WaS HaPPY
HOPPiNG MOroN Day.

Squidward Tentacles

**You'll never get what you want! You'll always let people step all over you! You're just like stairs!**

Plankton

259

# Above all, keep it cool.

SpongeBob SquarePants

LET'S CHANGE OUR NAMES TO WHY AND BOTHER.

SpongeBob SquarePants

**Does this mean we're not getting pizza?**

Patrick Star

# Could I have another hint?

Patrick Star

# Piece of cake!

SpongeBob SquarePants

I AM SO CONFUSED! MAYBE A
GOOD NIGHT'S SLEEP WILL HELP ME GET
MY HEAD ON STRAIGHT.

SpongeBob SquarePants

As if the answers to all your problems
will fall right out of the sky!

Squidward Tentacles

274

# CORRECT!

Plankton

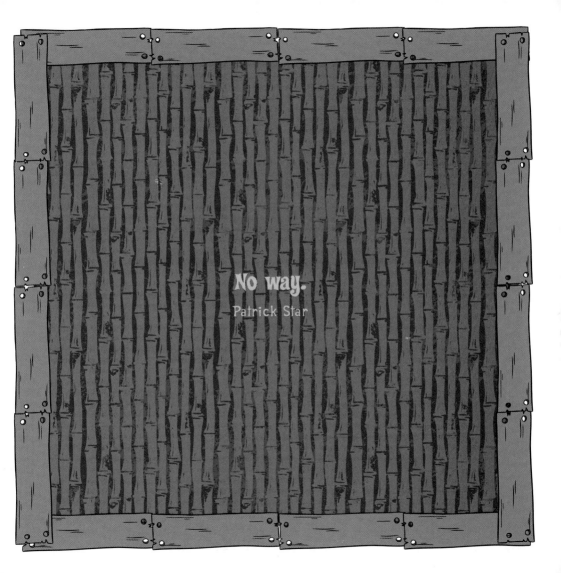

I'm sure there's another way.

SpongeBob SquarePants

Don't bother!

Squidward Tentacles

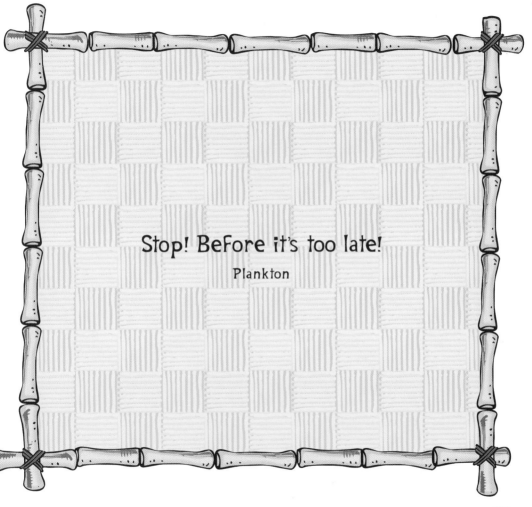

Stop! Before it's too late!

Plankton

YOU SHOULD BE ASHAMED OF YOURSELF.

Squidward Tentacles

We don't know.

SpongeBob SquarePants and Patrick Star